THE RIDING SCHOOL

by

C. P. MANDARA

Published by **CHIMERA**
ISBN 9781780807966

To the Aftermath of Dreams, which are always in colour.

CHAPTER ONE
Late for an Important Date

Jenny was late. That was one of the perks of being the daughter of Michael Redcliff, the millionaire oil tycoon; it meant you could get away with almost anything. Today she was late for riding classes.

Normally, an instructor would visit their stables and tutor her one-on-one. On this particular day, she had been ousted from her bed at a ludicrously early hour and packed off to the countryside. Her father had personally recommended the Albrecht Stables, which had meant she'd had to journey for four hours in his personal limo, to the depths of Lincolnshire, for a week's instructor training. She hadn't wanted to come and had no intention of actually becoming an instructor in the arts of horsemanship, far too fond of lazing in bed until midday and then shopping and partying until the wee hours of the morning. Her father had insisted that she take this course, however, mainly due to the fact that his mistress was arriving tomorrow and he had wanted the house to himself. He'd threatened to cut her allowance if she didn't attend, so there hadn't been a choice in the matter.

Staring out of the window, whilst sipping Crystal, Jenny thought her week was going to be one of the most boring on record. She was to lodge at the Pony Rides Hotel and by all accounts the nightlife nearby was not some of the most exhilarating. There was always the possibility that a cute guy would be taking the course but if that failed, she'd probably play hooky and sneak back down to London. She'd lifted her father's credit card from his wallet before leaving and as he had so many, there was little chance of him noticing.

'We're here, Miss Redcliff,' a nod from the driver.

'You've got to be kidding me,' said Jenny, her mouth dropping in horror. The Pony Rides Hotel looked like something out of *Anne of Green Gables*. The building featured traditional wood panels, ornate woodwork and looked ridiculously old-fashioned. Whoever named the hotel should be shot, she thought, because already she was imagining snotty-nosed children running around, yelling and screaming or demanding ice-cream.

Without a word of thanks Jenny waited for the chauffeur to open her door and carry her bags, all eight of them, to the reception desk. She took her own sweet time, admiring her reflection in a monogrammed silver compact mirror, before sauntering casually inside.

There was no-one at the reception desk when she entered, which gave her a few moments to look around. The hotel was surprisingly quiet, the only noise being traditional piped music from the internal stereo system and the rustle of papers from the office directly behind the desk. There was an almost overpowering smell of wood polish, which explained the glossy wood floors below her, which strangely didn't seem to have a single mark upon them. At least they valued cleanliness, Jenny thought. Exploring further, she found several sparkling silver trophies which were mounted in a glass display case located at the back of the hotel lobby and walls which appeared to be adorned with an impressive array of riding crops and some very unusual leather tack. Stepping forward to take a closer look, she was interrupted by the receptionist who had returned to her post at the desk.

'Oh, hello there,' said a very cultured voice, appearing surprised at having a guest waiting for her.

This must be some hotel, thought Jenny, if it was a shock every time a guest walked in. Wrinkling her nose in distaste she handed over her reservation number.

Running a manicured finger down the paperwork quickly, the receptionist lifted her head slowly and stared at Jenny directly. 'I'm sorry no-one was here to greet you but your check-in time appears to have been three hours ago.' There was a frown, some frantic fingernail tapping and a pause.

Jenny rolled her eyes in disgust. What sort of hotel was this? 'Look,' she said, 'have you got a room for me or not?'

The elegantly-coiffed receptionist seemed taken aback for a minute, as if she didn't normally deal with complaints, but recovered her composure swiftly. 'Oh we have lots of room for you, Miss Redcliff. Let me just see if I can get a few things rescheduled and we'll get you checked in promptly. Please take a seat.' She didn't wait for a thank you, which was just as well, as none appeared forthcoming.

Pouting and already bored with the day's events so far, Jenny took a seat and sighed loudly. The receptionist was speaking into her telephone and made no notion of having heard her. Twiddling the Tiffany locket she wore in her fingertips, she wondered if she shouldn't ring one of her friends and have them rescue her. She had already decided the week was going to be intolerably dull, there would be nothing except horses for entertainment and as of yet, she hadn't seen a bar. What did people do here after the day's training? Eat and go to bed? There was something else she'd noticed too: the restaurant had no Michelin star. They probably served up soggy fish and chips and if you were lucky you might get a three day old gooey mass of bread and butter pudding for dessert. Jenny grimaced. She had just entered Hell for a week, she was sure of it.

When the receptionist beckoned for her to come over not five minutes later, Jenny could barely conceal her jaded look.

'The ladies are ready for you now, Miss Redcliff, just take the black door over by the potted palm and they'll meet you on the other side.' The receptionist handed Jenny some paperwork. 'You'll need to take this with you.'

Sighing again and wondering why she couldn't just have been given a room key, Jenny pointed to the chauffer and asked, 'Where should he put my luggage?' She had no idea what the man was called.

'Ah, no need to worry about that, we'll take care of it, Miss Redcliff,' came the very efficient answer and with a nod, the receptionist smiled and released the chauffeur from any additional duties. He wasted no time in leaving the premises, having already had more than enough of the younger Redcliff's whinging and whining for one day.

'I hope you have a lovely stay with us,' offered the receptionist, but Jenny had already flounced past her and had begun to pull open the heavy, black, oak-panelled door.

CHAPTER TWO

The Tack Room

Jenny wasn't sure what she was expecting when she opened the door, but it certainly wasn't two old ladies chatting away at the end of a long, unlit and rather austere corridor. Peering down at the paperwork in her hands, she attempted to read the small text but found it was impossible in the dim light.

'Hello,' she ventured, but the pair at the end of the hall continued chatting animatedly and after trying an additional time, Jenny finally decided she'd had just about enough of this treatment. Did they have any idea who they were dealing with? 'Hello,' she said yet again, but this time much more sharply and was rewarded as both ladies turned around to stare at her, mouths open wide. What was it with the people around here? Maybe they were all completely insane, having lived in the country for far too long.

Finally, mouths snapping shut, the ladies turned around to face her and smiled. The oldest one, who had greying hair in a bun of which fizzy ends threatened to escape at any opportunity, began to speak.

'Hello there, dearie, you must be Miss Redcliff I'm thinking. Well, let me introduce myself. My name is Agnes and this here,' she pointed to her portly colleague, 'is Henrietta. We'll just need to take a few measurements from you in order to get you started. It's a real shame you're late because you could be out in the paddock by now having fun with all the other fillies if you'd turned up just a smidgeon earlier. Ah well, can't be helped. Traffic was it?'

'Something like that,' murmured Jenny, when it had in fact been a leisurely breakfast at one of London's most expensive dining establishments followed by a spa detour involving a manicure, pedicure and hour long aromatherapy massage.

Henrietta nodded. 'Well, if you would just like to follow us for a moment, we'll get you back on tack in a jiffy.' She laughed at her own joke.

Jenny was beginning to think the staff at this hotel were either completely mad, or very nearly. Fillies in fields? Back on tack? Was it possible they were living in an alternate universe?

Henrietta, her red hair pinned up with numerous coloured pencils which stuck out at random angles, ushered Jenny inside a room which had *Pony Tack* emblazoned across the door in red and black antique lettering. There was so much leather inside, it wasn't as if you were going to mistake the room for any other use, thought Jenny wryly as she walked through the open door. Interestingly, there was a bizarre brown leather horse contraption centred in the middle of the room with leather straps of varying sizes hanging off it at different intervals. What on earth was that used for? As if that wasn't enough, there were literally hundreds of shiny black leather bits in a large cardboard box to the far left, another box housed an impressive stack of black and orange rubber balls and yet another box was filled with yards and yards of coarse long black hair.

'What do you think?' asked Henrietta, who was smiling broadly and displaying a rather yellowed set of teeth. 'It's lovely isn't it? Our tack comes from all around the world and some choice pieces take over three months to make. Have a good look around and do let me know if there is anything in particular you'd like. Oh, can I just have a look at your paperwork, sweetie?'

Jenny barely heard her as her gaze had settled on a row of wooden shelving at the front of the room containing leather circlets. Were they collars? As Henrietta held out a hand for the paperwork, she handed it over silently. They weren't collars for horses because they were far too small. Some of the collars were very deep in width; some were barely a centimetre wide; others featured metal spikes, large D-rings and ropes of silver chain in several degrees of thickness and length. The collars were made in colours ranging through white, yellow, blue, green, coral, red and black. Spinning around to the rear of the room, nervous adrenaline beginning to pump through her body, she noted both black leather and PVC boots, most of which were knee-high with the remainder being so long they had to be thigh high. Most featured intricate lacing and gleaming metal eyelets, had platform heels of at least five centimetres in height and a few even contained metal 'U' shaped horseshoes on the underside of the sole. Her eyes began to bulge in their sockets as reality began to set in. This was not a tack room for horses. All of this equipment had been designed with humans in mind!

'I, ah, think there has been some kind of mistake,' said Jenny rather breathlessly as she angled her body to the door, spying leather cuffs and black pony masks hanging above the frame.

Agnes gave her colleague a narrowed look. 'What does the paperwork say under "status", Henrietta?'

'Hmm,' Henrietta hadn't been paying much attention to Jenny until now, sorting through a box of bridles and martingales that had become tangled on her bench, but a quick look up at her latest trainee had her eyes frantically searching the page in front of her for the required information. 'It says "Subject has not been notified".'

Jenny had just at that moment found an enormously large collection of rubber ovals, tapering at both ends and rather fat in the middle. She was not a complete idiot. She'd browsed through sex catalogues on occasion and was fairly certain that these were what were termed as 'butt plugs'. Alarmingly, quite a few of them had long black tails attached to their flat end. That was enough to send her over the edge. In the next instant she screamed and dashed for the door.

'We have a bolter,' said Agnes. 'Batten down the hatches.'

CHAPTER THREE
Silenced and Measured for Size

Henrietta was already ahead of her, having pressed a button by her bench which slammed the door shut and locked it. It had come in useful on more than one occasion. Not all the occupants at this facility were willing, but they all had one thing in common. They paid a very large sum of money to be here. Exactly how much depended on their circumstances, but Henrietta managed in one glance to see the figure of £500,000 standing out on the form in bold black numbers. It seemed that Mr Redcliff really, *really*, wanted his daughter to get the full works.

Agnes grabbed one of Jenny's arms and let Henrietta take the other. They'd practised the move many times before and, as usual, it went like clockwork. Mind you, they'd not come across anyone with a black belt in Karate yet, so there was always the possibility that a filly might escape one day. It was very unlikely, but not impossible. Unfortunately for Jenny, she had no such training in martial arts. As soon as Henrietta bent one of her arms around behind her back and up towards her neck, the pain nearly crippled her and she almost fell to her knees.

'There, there, dearie. Play nicely and we'll not have to use those sorts of tactics on you again,' Agnes said in a soothing tone. Agnes didn't think much of doling out pain; she left that to the various Mistresses and Masters who made the very act an art form. Agnes was in this job because she loved leather and because the pay was extremely good. She intended to have a retirement home in the south of France in a couple of years, hopefully complete with a fully trained pony of her own.

Henrietta took one look at Agnes and rolled her eyes. The old dear was daydreaming yet again. 'Agnes, Agnes!'

Agnes shook her head momentarily. 'Hmm?'

'I thought we might let our new filly take a brief rest. What say you?' Henrietta eyed the horse purposefully.

'Oh, good idea, Hetty,' said Agnes, immediately following her train of thought and together they began to pull Jenny in the direction of the leather horse.

Jenny was not going to have any of that. Kicking and clawing, scratching and biting, she let out a scream that could have broken all the windows in the neighbouring village. It didn't do her any good. Agnes simply yanked the arm she had imprisoned back upwards and Henrietta lifted the girl off her feet and tried to gently deposit her on the horse. With a straggle of limbs doing the spaghetti dance, it didn't work quite the way it was intended and Jenny landed on her back with rather a good thump. If it were possible, the screaming intensified.

The ladies wasted no time applying the straps which would hold the trainee down. Agnes took care of her ankles, making neat loops with the leather and yanking them tight until they were aligned with the legs of the horse. Henrietta worked at more than twice the speed, managing two arms, a body strap around the waist, one around the neck and another circling the forehead. Reaching down to pull a lever beneath the horse, she split the bottom half in two, splaying Jenny's legs neatly. The trainee's movement was now limited to around two inches of leeway from one side to the other. Pulling one of the pencils out of her unruly chignon, she made sure that the width of the pencil could easily be fitted inside each restraint. They took safety very seriously at the Pony Rides Hotel and she wasn't going to be the first to lose a victim by choking them accidentally. 'We're good,' she finally announced, having to yell over the screeching noise Jenny will still making.

Agnes tossed Hetty some wax earplugs and applied her own. They wouldn't need them in a few moments, but measurements had to be taken and it was murder on your eardrums to listen to that kind of noise for any length of time. She then proceeded to get out her tape measure and bending over Jenny's face began to measure the exact length of her lips. The trainee tried to bite her, which was expected and Hetty responded by giving her a sharp, stinging slap which stilled her movements for long enough to get the required information. It looked as though this one would require the petite selection of rubber bit gags, which was quite unusual and might even make her highly prized if someone managed to train her properly. Agnes wrote the details down in her notebook and added a tongue port for good measure. A tongue port was a great piece of kit which fitted over the bit gag and ensured that a) no intelligible speech would be heard from the pony and b) it prevented the pony's tongue from playing with the bit in any way. She suspected the lucky trainer would need all the help they could get in the mastering of this filly. Taking measurements around Jenny's head for bridle, blinker and blindfold attachments, she quickly finished her notes and began rummaging around in the drawer next to her. Spotting a small orange ball gag with a simple black leather strap, she wasted no time pressing it into Jenny's lips.

Unsurprisingly Jenny didn't let the invasive object in willingly and it was Hetty who pinched her nostrils together and waited for her to draw breath, which in turn allowed Agnes to apply enough pressure to push the ball inside her mouth. The strap was quickly fastened around her head by means of a single buckle. All screaming abruptly ceased, to be replaced with a muffled groaning noise of a much more acceptable volume. As if frustrated by the lack of noise she was able to make, the trainee increased her struggles to virtually no effect with the tight restraints binding her.

Fishing her earplugs out and throwing them in the general direction of the bin, Hetty sighed. 'That's better. Are you getting the scissors out or am I?' she asked. Agnes didn't reply. Shaking her head, she tapped her on the arm and pointed to her ears. Agnes got the message.

'Sorry Hetty, did you say something?'

'I said, are you getting the scissors or shall I?' Henrietta made cutting motions with her fingers.

'Oh, right. I'll do it and you can write down the details, if that's all right. Hetty didn't bother to respond, searching around for her pencil which had somehow disappeared. Pulling out another one from her hair, she frowned as a curly red tendril flopped onto her cheek. Eyeing it with displeasure she said, 'I need a haircut.'

Agnes picked up a pair of dressmaking shears and raised her eyebrows enquiringly.

'From a professional, dear,' said Hetty in response. 'Now get to work, no dillydallying. We're off schedule by three hours already, heaven help us if we delay the lass any further. Her ass will be redder than a strawberry.'

Agnes didn't need to be told twice and began cutting through the fabric of Jenny's jeans, starting from the bottom and working her way up. She cut a long slice through the entire left side of the jeans and then began on the right, humming as she did so.

Jenny was almost positive this had to be a nightmare. If it wasn't, her dad would be notified soon enough and would make sure these idiots paid handsomely for their mistake. This sort of thing didn't happen in this day and age. She had rights. She wanted a lawyer and a very heavy baseball bat, not necessarily in that order. Tied down to the table and gagged, she was only just holding herself together. Please, dear God, she prayed, don't let it get any worse. That was before they started cutting away her clothes.

The jeans slid off easily in two sections and Agnes let them drop to the floor. That just left brown ankle boots, some socks and a pair of black lace panties to dispose of on her lower half. The first two were removed by hand and the panties melted under the pressure of the sharp steel blade. The top half was considerably easier, consisting of just an angora sweater and a matching black lace bra. The glinting scissors slid effortlessly through wool and lace, leaving the subject of their attentions swiftly naked.

Anger had replaced shock in Jenny's face. Did they not know that her designer jeans cost over four hundred pounds? The sweater was closer to eight hundred and would be impossible to replace as it was one of a kind. She wanted to gouge their eyes out. How dare they? Struggling futilely at the thick brown straps that bound her, Jenny tried hard to make her concerns known, but the sound that came out was nothing more than a croak. It took some moments to realise that ruined designer clothes were the least of her worries. She was naked, she was gagged and she was wide open for a reason. A tendril of fear began to take root.

'She really is quite pretty, don't you think?' said Agnes, her tape measure back in her fingers once more.

Henrietta paused and took a good long look at the trainee before her. 'She's not bad, I suppose, with her long black hair, deep blue eyes, raspberry-tinted lips and long, thick eyelashes. Then if you take the clear ivory flesh into account, small but perfectly proportioned breasts, blush-coloured areola and pussy lips, then yes, I suppose she could fetch quite a sum if properly trained.' Hetty turned to Agnes who was daydreaming once more. 'But don't get your hopes up, Aggie, she's far too feisty to ever achieve the black. She'll be lucky to manage the green.'

Agnes sighed heartily. 'There goes my bonus.' Both ladies were awarded a bonus on the final training report of the slaves they outfitted. The more accurately a slave was outfitted, supposedly, the better colour collar they could achieve. Between them they had never managed more than the coral and each collar upwards from white doubled the bonus in size. 'I'm telling you, Hetty, I need to retire soon. My bones need sunshine.'

'Hurry up and get to work, Agnes. We're on a timescale here.' Hetty poised her pencil above her pad and waited expectantly. In a matter of seconds she was scribbling furiously. Measurements for martingales, reins, saddles, corsets, bodysuits, chambons, cross ties, hobbles, surcingles, polo wraps, tails and the obligatory saddle. Then it was time for the ladies to discuss the materials they would need, the stitching, the colours, the finish and the required quantity of each item. As there were no monetary restraints for this particular pony, it was a more enjoyable task than usual.

'She's going to look gorgeous, when she's all trussed up and ready to trot,' sighed Henrietta.

Jenny tried to make as much noise as she could through the rubber ball, whilst struggling madly. She managed nothing more than a muffled grunt and about an inch of leverage with the leather straps that were clearly not going to give, no matter how much she pulled at them. Meanwhile, the cold tape measure wrapped itself around her body again and again. These people, whoever they were, were talking as if she didn't even exist. She was Jenny, she was not a filly, she was not a pony and she was certainly not going to be an animal for someone's entertainment.

She'd listened to the long list of tack items that were being discussed in horror. Knowing what each piece was used for on a real horse and having most of the items readily on display here in the human tack room had just about turned her insides to liquid. For instance, she knew that a chambon was used to control the carriage of a horse's head and that cross ties would ensure a horse stayed relatively straight and upright, making sure there was no fidgeting or turning. Hobbles, as the name suggested, would prevent kicking and restrict all but the smallest of movements. Surcingles circled the waist and enabled the trainer to teach proper head carriage, whilst polo wraps were basically leggings for horses, providing a degree of protection to the wearer. She could not be forced to wear any of this, could she? Trying to slow her breathing and think sensibly, she reasoned that there must be some way out of this mess. Unfortunately, it was very hard to be reasonable when you were tied down without the use of your voice.

'I think we're ready for the internal, Hetty,' said Agnes, winding her tape measure in circles around her hand.

Internal what? Jenny thought in panic, already assuming the worst.

'Right ho, dearie,' said Hetty, searching for something in a squeaky wooden drawer.

Jenny's eyes didn't leave Henrietta as she watched her slowly pull two clear latex gloves out of a box with an audible snap. One by one she struggled with the rubber until she'd squeezed all her pudgy fingers inside. Cracking her knuckles slowly, she smiled at Jenny. It was supposed to be a reassuring look. The next words that came out of her lips were, 'Don't worry sweetheart, I'll be very gentle,' but they were wasted.

Jenny had fainted clean away.

CHAPTER FOUR

The Exam, Part I

'Oh Hetty, do you have to do that? You know it scares some of the newbies,' said Agnes reprovingly.

'Most of them enjoy it, Aggie, and let's face it, you need to let them know what's coming.'

'There are softer approaches you could take, especially with the fillies who haven't signed up for this particular type of training. You've scared the poor lass half to death. Now I'm going to have to get the first aid kit,' she said, frowning. 'Can you just release the door for me?'

She depressed the door release button and Agnes sprinted out. Well, what counted as sprinting for Agnes, which was in fact a very brisk walk. That gave Hetty plenty of time to get all the equipment ready that she would need to conduct her exam. The first thing she did was wheel a small, three-tiered metal trolley alongside the middle of the horse, parallel to Jenny's stomach. That was where most of the action would be. Stepping into a small box room, located just past the collars, she pulled on the light cord. Immediately the room came to life with row upon row of exquisitely-decorated glass dildos, shimmering silver jars of lubricant, ruled measuring dildos in sizes from tiny to enormous and inflating rubber dildos in various bold shades.

Hetty took particular pride in this room; it was she who had bought most of the items and did the yearly inventory. She had unwrapped, polished, cleaned, placed, cherished and put to use most of the equipment on display. Agnes nearly always let her do the exams, knowing how much she enjoyed them; horses for courses, as it were. In the days when she was known as Mistress Etta, she must have had one of the biggest toy boxes in the industry. She could cow submissives with just a glance back then. Chastity belts and chains, ah, those were the days.

Agnes popped her head through the door and waggled a green first aid kit in the air. 'Are you ready yet?' she asked.

'Give me five minutes and then you can wake sleeping beauty up. There's no point having her conscious before absolutely necessary.'

'No arguments here, I'll just finish my coffee and have a look through her paperwork.'

Hetty didn't bother to respond, already too absorbed in the tools around her. On her trolley she placed one gleaming pump action bottle of silky smooth lubricant, the thin version rather than the nasty, thick, sticky stuff. Next she added a twelve inch ruled glass dildo of the slimmest size available, and placed the medium next to it for good measure; she couldn't be running back and forth for things at her age. A black inflatable dildo followed and that completed the necessary equipment for the vaginal exam, bar a stainless steel speculum and some long cotton swabs. The rectal exam would follow with similar equipment, just much smaller in size. She brought the items back into the tack room and smiled when she saw that Agnes had brought back a couple of plastic tubs, one with warm water inside. Dropping the two speculums into the tub of water, she changed her gloves for a fresh pair and waited for the smelling salts to do their thing.

Agnes didn't have to wave the rather potent bottle of salts under Jenny's nose for long before her eyes snapped open. Then a gaggle of incoherent would-be screaming followed.

'She's all yours, Hetty.' Agnes picked up her notepad once more.

Jenny's eyes goggled as rubber-coated fingers began to exam her groin, brushing through her pubic hair to inspect the underlying skin beneath, pushing and pressing into the flesh, separating her labia majora and raising the hood of her clitoris to touch the little nub beneath. A moan escaped through her gag, she couldn't help herself. What on earth was wrong with her?

'A Brazilian wax definitely seems to be the fashion of choice at the moment,' commented Hetty, 'although I think you'll look much prettier when you've been properly readied for pony play and all that nasty hair is removed.'

Agnes nodded her head in agreement. 'It helps for your trainer to be able to see when you're aroused, too. There is nothing like a little pony that's hot to trot with glisteningly wet and swollen labia.'

Hetty squirted a thin trail of lubricant on two of her fingers before slowly parting her subject's inner lips and sliding them inside her vagina. She checked Jenny's uterus and ovaries and the surrounding skin for abnormalities, such as cysts or lesions. 'Right, that all seems to be fine.'

Taking the larger speculum out of the warm water, she dried it on a piece of clean white linen and slowly slid it into Jenny's vagina. It slid in easily but her patient began to struggle furiously once more.

Agnes put two fingers to the carotid artery on Jenny's neck and checked for her pulse. 'She's going into overdrive again. I think we need a little relaxant, if you know what I mean.'

Hetty smiled and withdrew the speculum slowly, placing it back in the water. 'A freebie? Hmm, well just this once, I suppose.' Hetty's thumb and fingers went back to their earlier position, separating the outer lips and pulling the hood of the clitoris back to expose its slightly swelling occupant. With her free hand she managed to squeeze a dollop of lubricant onto the tip of her index finger in a one-handed motion - it was amazing what you could do with years of practice - and applied light pressure to the tip of Jenny's clitoris. Just a few seconds of pressure and then she began slow, circular movements which teased the little nub into life.

Agnes came alongside to help with the ruled glass dildo. She rested it at the entrance of Jenny's vagina and applied light pressure. It wouldn't be able to slide in until its subject had become thoroughly aroused.

Hetty continued her attentions, light little taps, soft palpations and then a little bit harder, rubbing in quick concentric circles.

A long, thin line of dribble began to seep from Jenny's lips as she began to moan helplessly.

'I think our little pony likes to play,' said Agnes, winking at her colleague.

'Oh, I suspect she's played many times before. Her paperwork states that she brings home a different man nearly every day of the week and I suspect it's not business related. The forms state that our little pony here has never even managed to get a job, let alone hold one down, due to laziness mostly.'

'Well, laziness isn't a trait that will be tolerated here and I'm sure she'll soon mend her naughty ways,' said Agnes thoughtfully.

Jenny barely heard any of the conversation that was going on. Her buttocks had begun to bounce up and down on the leather horse with rhythmic frequency and her breasts were bouncing in unison with proudly erect, straining nipples. Heat had begun to pool within her face, turning it a deep shade of plum. She was beginning to breathe heavily through her nose and was clenching her fingers tightly inside her palms.

'Oh, we've got movement on the dildo,' said Agnes. It was beginning to slide quite comfortably inside the slippery lips placed before it and if possible, Jenny went a shade darker in colour as she felt the cold glass begin to penetrate. Whilst Henrietta continued to masturbate the trainee, Agnes gave the dildo a little more pressure in encouragement and was rewarded when it began to sink inside its occupant.

'Six inches and counting, Hetty,' she said.

Hetty now placed two fingers upon Jenny's clitoris and intensified the speed of movement.

'Seven inches.'

Agnes began to pump the dildo in and out as Jenny raised her backside off the leather. 'She's going to make the most wonderful pony girl. Just look at the expression on her face.'

Hetty turned her attention back to her subject's face and was quite surprised to see a meek little submissive, almost ashamed of the orgasm she was about to have, panting and heaving for breath whilst nearly foaming at the mouth. Indeed she looked quite tortured in the throes of passion and any Master would be extremely pleased with that particular look during training. Hetty's fingers found their final rhythm and with a measured pressure, they would send the pony girl off to 'O' land in a few seconds.

'Eight inches and we're stopping. It won't budge any further,' said Agnes.

'She'll need to work on that. Eight inches won't do at all.'

Agnes nodded.

Jenny tried to scream yet again. This time it would have been a full throttle scream of pleasure had it been able to escape. As it was it was pretty impressive, and had another line of saliva dripping down her cheek to pool on the floor beneath her. As her pussy began to convulse around the dildo she rode wave after wave of the strong contractions that had assailed her body before a fit of trembling overtook her. No-one had said a word the entire time and nor had anyone looked at her face. It should have been a very cold, dispassionate experience, and yet that had not been the case at all.

Agnes slowly slid the glass dildo back out again and placed it in the used receptacle box. 'Your turn again,' she said.

The shiny, black, inflatable dildo was picked up and admired. It would be used to measure what kind of width the trainee would be able to manage comfortably on her initial training. Hetty licked her lips and covered the black plastic in lubricant. The penis-shaped inflatable was then slowly inserted inside Jenny, who at the moment appeared rather desensitized to all that was going on around her. The new dildo barely needed the aid of lubricant, sliding deeply inside its victim with little additional help needed. When Hetty was confident that she had inserted it as far as it was able to go she began to use the small oval-shaped pump which was attached to the dildo by a black quarter-inch tube.

'Let me know when you feel a little pressure, Jenny,' said Hetty, but Jenny still looked mindless with pleasure and made no acknowledgment. One pump, then two, four, six and finally on the seventh pump of air Jenny began to protest in little staccato bursts, having finally snapped out of the aftermath of her delicious orgasm.

'Jot down an inch and a half, Aggie,' said Hetty, who was now deflating the pump and slowly sliding the much slimmer dildo back out. A loud clunk announced that the inflatable dildo had joined its friend in the used box and would no longer be needed.

Jenny was feeling intense heat in her cheeks and embarrassment curled itself all the way through her body. Not only had she just orgasmed in front of these two old ladies, who happened to be complete strangers, but she had enjoyed herself. No, make that *really* enjoyed herself. She had never had an orgasm like it. It had ripped through her body with such force that she had screamed out loud without even realising it. Not one of the men she had sex with, and there had been a few, had managed anything even remotely close to that kind of tumultuous eruption. What was wrong with her? Wake up, she told herself, you must snap out of this weird dreamworld you have managed to create. Although she had a suspicious feeling that not even her subconscious could come up with something this bizarre.

A knock sounded on the door. It was loud, insistent and the owner of such a knock obviously did not want to be ignored.

'Come in,' both ladies chorused together.

A male head popped around the door frame. 'Hello, Aggie, Hetty,' he nodded to each and gave a rather dazzlingly bright white smile. 'Just to let you know I'll be in charge of the trainee filly when you're done. I've been told in no uncertain terms that we need to show a firm hand with her at all times. Apparently she is what's termed as "difficult" but we'll give her the benefit of the doubt until her training begins.' He winked at Jenny.

Jenny tried instinctively to cover herself up, acutely aware of how naked and exposed she was. Of course the effort was pointless. All of the most intimate parts of her body were on display and he didn't even bat an eyelid. To make matters worse, the man was drop dead 'I've died and gone to heaven' gorgeous. He had a posh English accent, short black hair gelled upwards in soft spikes and chocolate-brown eyes. If that wasn't enough, add tight white riding breeches, a white shirt, a pair of black knee-high boots and a matching riding coat. Most women would have melted into a small puddle before him and she was definitely one of them. He was quite possibly the most desirable man she had ever had the good fortune to lay her eyes upon and she had to meet him like this. Life was not fair. A groan of frustration left her lips as her body began to heat once more, blood pumping furiously through her. Oh no, she thought, this cannot be happening yet again. Gritting her teeth she tried to quell her reaction.

'Did you want to help perform the exam, Master Mark?' asked Hetty.

Jenny tried to shake her head in horror, knowing that as soon as the man's fingers touched her she would explode. It had been bad enough being observed by the two old ladies, but having an attractive man there to witness these depravities would make it ten times worse. With all her might she willed him to say no.

'Well,' he paused, as if thinking for a moment, 'how about I sit over here in the corner and watch? If you need a hand with anything you can let me know.' The devilish smile he gave to the ladies indicated that he knew his presence would give an added torment to their victim.

Jenny tried to thrash about on the horse to let her feelings on the matter be known, but other than her bottom sliding around on the leather which was now slick with her own juices, there wasn't much movement of any account and no-one paid the slightest bit of attention to her.

In a few brief seconds Mark had settled himself quietly on a wooden stool that would give him the best view of everything that would shortly be happening between Jenny's legs. Hetty, meanwhile, had grabbed the larger steel speculum out of the water again and was slowly patting it dry with clean linen.

'There, there, horsie,' said Hetty, who had watched Jenny's attempted protest with amusement. 'Most of the fillies around here would kill for a few minutes of Master Mark's time. Give him a few hours and I'm sure you'll be drooling at the mouth along with the rest of them.'

That was exactly what Jenny was afraid of.

CHAPTER FIVE
The Exam, Part II

The speculum slid into Jenny in one single motion. Most of that was due to the added presence of Mark, who had made her so wet that her body was practically 'gushing' with enthusiasm. It was mortifying and there was nothing she could do to control her reaction. As the blades of the speculum pulled at her inner walls and stretched them, she felt herself being opened and displayed for these three strangers and it wasn't as unpleasant as it should have been. Jenny was aroused. She knew Mark's eyes were upon her most intimate parts and it made her hot; breathlessly, heart-poundingly and deliciously hot. She squirmed.

'Interesting reaction,' said a deep male voice.

'I think most of it is down to you,' said Agnes, who couldn't help a smile.

Hetty picked up a long cotton swab and bending over Jenny's torso, all the buttons on her starched white linen shirt straining, took a sample of cells from Jenny's cervix. She talked as she worked, letting her patient know exactly what was happening. 'We're just checking for any abnormalities or lesions. The sample of cells I've just collected will be sent to our laboratory and if there's anything that concerns the technician then your Master or Mistress will be notified and will take it from there.'

That was when Jenny started to realise that all control was going to be taken from her. If she'd contracted cancer, she wasn't going to be the first to know. Until she could arrange her escape ticket out of here, her life was no longer her own. To say it was a sobering thought was something of an understatement.

The speculum was slowly closed and extracted.

'Right,' said Hetty, 'we'd better get started on the rectal exam. Can you get me some cushions, Aggie?'

As soon as she heard those words a new wave of rebellion swept its way through Jenny and she renewed her struggles with vigour. She had never before been touched in that particular part of her anatomy and she certainly didn't want to start in this room, with these complete strangers watching over her. She would not stand for this. Helplessly, she watched as Aggie plumped up two large, overstuffed cotton cushions and placed them under the small of her back. This had the effect of thrusting her bottom into the air, giving a much better degree of access for whoever chose to perform the exam. Struggling had no effect and the cushions would not be moved.

'What does it say on the form for anal, Aggie?'

Agnes consulted the paperwork on her desk again. 'Unknown.'

'Have you ever had anal sex before, Jenny?' Henrietta asked softly.

Jenny shook her head as fast and as hard as she was able.

A soft male chuckle served to further humiliate her.

'I think she's going to be very popular around here,' said Mark, trying to suppress a grin.

'My, oh my,' said Aggie with awe, 'an anal virgin. We haven't had one of those in years and years.'

All Hetty did was grunt in response. 'I have a feeling I'm going to need some help with this. Would you keep her distracted for a moment or two, Master Mark?'

'It would be my absolute pleasure,' came the immediate response.

It eventually occurred to Jenny that wriggling about like an anaconda was going to give everyone more of a show, rather than less. So by sheer force of will she managed to stop herself squirming madly, but only just.

'May I take out her gag?' Mark looked to Hetty for an answer.

'You are the ruling authority here,' she replied, 'but I thank you for asking. Feel free to do as you please with the trainee.' Hetty thought for a moment. 'She's going to need a "breaking in" session later, if she has any chance at all of wearing a tail tomorrow. Would you like us to leave a little *present* inside her, if you catch my drift?' She smiled innocently.

'I think she would like that,' said Mark.

Jenny wasn't at all sure that she would. No-one was touching her down there and as soon as Mark removed her gag they were going to find out just what she thought of them all, and it wasn't going to be particularly polite.

'Right, I'm going to remove your gag on two conditions,' said Mark, which immediately focused Jenny's attention. 'One, no biting. Two, no talking unless spoken to. Nod if you understand these conditions and agree to comply with them.'

Jenny was no fool and nodded her head quickly.

'Just for clarity's sake, there are three good reasons you'll do exactly as you've been told: there is a riding crop attached to my belt and I am itching to use it. Two, I bite harder, and three, you are going to spend the next three or four hours in my company and I am a Master at torture, amongst other equally unpleasant things that you may not want to find out about on your first day with us. Are we clear?'

Jenny nodded. She'd take her chances where she could find them, threats or no threats. Besides, no-one would dare mess with Jenny Redcliff, when they found out who she was and what her father was capable of.

When the gag came out it made an embarrassingly loud sucking noise and left a long trail of saliva from her mouth to the trolley, which was where he placed it. He broke the connection and before she had a chance to voice all the rather pressing concerns she had at the top of her lungs, he took her lips in a brutal and punishing kiss. He literally sucked all the air from her body and it was... electric. He licked, nipped and even gave her bottom lip a small bite and she *loved* it. Gone were all thoughts of stamping her feet, screaming and shouting with rage, or contacting a lawyer. In their place was an escalating need which was increasing by the second.

Mark's eyes watched as Hetty reached for the smaller speculum and he gave a tiny shake of his head. That wasn't going to be happening today. They would be lucky to get a measurement. It wouldn't pose a problem. All ponies had regulation visits to the vet and she would get her fair share of attention then. He picked up the slimmest-ruled dildo on the trolley and handed it to the gloved fingers which were still hovering in midair. She nodded silently and covered it in as much lubricant as possible.

When the cold, slippery glass dildo was placed at the entrance to her anal passage, the shock was evident in Jenny's eyes. She did not want to be touched down there. Another round of frantic struggling ensued, but the dildo remained irritatingly in place and no amount of wriggling would shift it. It didn't matter because Jenny had clenched her sphincter so tight that they'd be lucky to get a matchstick near her. She was not going to let down her guard.

Mark's eyes had a knowing gleam in them. It wasn't a secret that he preferred it when the trainees played hardball. Give him obstinate, unruly, rude, sarcastic, narcissistic or greedy any day. They were a lot more fun to tame than the 'Miss Goody Two Shoes' variety. Jenny was definitely not going to fall under the latter category and that was so much the better. She already had him smiling. Now that he'd pulled away from her lips he could see her gritted teeth and narrowed eyes. She believed she would be able to deny them entry just by tightly tensing her body. The girl had a lot to learn. He whispered in her ear.

'That long glass dildo is going to be filling your ass as far as it can

19

possibly go whether you wish it or not. Not only that, but in a few short weeks you are going to beg to be fucked in that hole or indeed any hole your trainer may choose. You will have to beg for the privilege of serving your Master or Mistress and perhaps, if you are lucky, to earn a rare moment of release. One of the things that all pony girls or boys have in common is that their asses are rarely left unplugged. That's why you'll need a "breaking in" session. At the moment you'll only be able to take the tiniest of plugs, which means your tail will be of a very unimpressive thickness and length. Your trainer will work with you every day until that beautiful backside can hold the weight of a proper horse's tail inside it. Every single moment you wear it, when you feel the coarse hair tickling your inner thighs or feel the plug vibrating inside your body, it will remind you of your status. As of now, you are an animal. There will be no speech, no clothes and no conscious will of your own. Ponies are no longer seen as human and your sole purpose in life will be to please your owner. You would do well to remember that.'

The words that dripped inside Jenny's ear made her go cold with fear. She had little time to dwell on them though, before his fingers began to torment her body. They were skilled, expert fingers that knew exactly how to play a woman; a soft brush on the underside of a breast, a light caress down the length of an inner thigh, a flick of a fingernail against the tender point of a nipple or a slow, sensuous lick following the curve of the neck. It didn't matter where his fingers landed as they had more magic in them than a witch on All Hallows' Eve. They made her gasp, shiver, tingle and burn. She was supposed to be screaming, shouting and demanding her release, but the spell she was under had her body coiled with tension and her mouth moaning in pleasure. Try as she might, she couldn't snap herself out of the sensual haze that had befallen her.

'You're not going to give in that easily are you?' asked Mark, raising his eyebrows in challenge. 'I thought you were going to prove a tough little filly to tame and yet here we have a purring pussycat.' His fingers gave her clit the lightest of strokes, that tiny pressure nearly all that was needed to send her over the edge before nodding to Hetty, who, in one swift motion, breached the tightly clenched inner anal walls to lodge the measuring dildo inside her back passage.

Jenny's orgasm died an instant death as the pain of having her anal walls dilated took hold. She shrieked and bucked and shrieked some more for good measure. It took another hard, brutal kiss and vigorous pressure on her clit before the noise subsided. She could feel her sphincter convulsing madly around the foreign object lodged inside it. It was not welcome, but that didn't stop her tormentor. Hetty twisted and turned the thin, cylindrical glass rule inside her and urged it forward. Jenny tried to stop the dildo's insidious movement, but squirming with all her might just seemed to encourage it to slip more deeply inside her, so she stopped even that small token of protest. Compressing her lips together, she gave Mark a baleful glance, eyes flashing pure malice. If he wanted his lips anywhere near hers he'd better be prepared to do battle.

'Now that's what I'm talking about,' said Mark, as the corner of his lip began to twitch in amusement. He turned his attention to Hetty, still carefully poised over Jenny's groin. 'How far have you managed to get?'

'Three inches, Master Mark,' came the somewhat concerned reply.

She had a right to be concerned, for that wouldn't do at all, thought Mark. The bigger the eventual plug a pony could take would affect her value considerably and you weren't going to manage a great tail with just three inches to play around with. Time would tell if it was going to pose a problem and the first few weeks of training would be crucial. Still, he suspected that Hetty had given up a little too soon. 'Would you mind if I have a go?' he asked.

Hetty shook her head and smiled. She was more than happy to let an expert take charge and she had a feeling that Mark would achieve more success than she. The man ratcheted up female heart rates by just breathing. She held the rule in place until Mark had closed his fingers around it and then took a seat next to Agnes.

Jenny did not want Mark anywhere near her ass or anywhere near her at all for that matter. She finally managed to find her voice. 'I demand you release me this instant! Do you know who my father is? He'll have you all arrested the second he realises I've been kid...' her tirade stopped almost as quickly as it had started. There were two fingers pumping up and down in her slippery wet channel, a mouth and tongue doing a flawless tango on her clit and yet more stimulation as the dildo twisted, turned and pumped mercilessly inside her. Jenny's voice died in her throat. She could not have another orgasm in front of all these people. Not like this. Desperately trying to quell her feelings of intense arousal by thinking of everyday mundane things such as painting her nails, cleaning her teeth or sitting through her French lessons, she reasoned that eventually her body would come back down to earth.

Mark watched her battle for control with interest. His perceptive glance missed nothing and he was thoroughly enjoying watching her lips as they silently mouthed a decidedly eclectic mix of French vocabulary. The poor lass didn't stand a chance. He had just found her G-spot and was beginning to torment the area with consummate ease. Watching the trainee's body light up like a Christmas tree, Mark stared at her pretty little face as flames of anguish engulfed her. She couldn't lift a finger to stop him and neither could she curb her reaction. To be fair, even the most skilled in restraint would have a hard job resisting the mechanisms he employed.

'No, no, no,' Jenny whispered, even as her body cried out exactly the opposite. She was fighting her reaction with everything she possessed, but it was like trying to stopper a storm drain with a bath plug - pointless. The floodgates had been opened and the room was filled with her scent. It was the heavy, musky, sweet smell of arousal and it was getting stronger by the second. Her legs were sticky and wet, her body strained against the leather straps and she was already trembling violently.

Mark's lips stopped his ministrations on her clit to speak. 'We have six inches, Aggie. That'll do.'

He slipped the dildo smoothly out of her ass with an audible pop and there was a quick scratch of pen on paper before the room went silent once more. Then footsteps; loud, heavy footsteps which she guessed were Henrietta's. The next thing she knew Mark's face was pressed against her ear and he whispered.

'Do you want to beg for release, horsie?' His words were like a red rag to a bull.

'Fu...uuuu,' came Jenny's response, which would have been much clearer had Henrietta not just squeezed her jaw open and forced the orange ball securely back in place.

'We'll have none of that nastiness here, dearie,' said Henrietta disapprovingly, in her sternest voice.

Mark laughed and gave the trainee a pointed look. 'I'll take that as a no, shall I? You'll live to regret that decision.'

Finding a new burst of energy Jenny shook her head, trying to indicate that she would not, but his face had already disappeared once more, disturbingly between her legs. Once again his tongue found her clit and this time he sucked. It produced a much tighter friction than the licking, and the sensation quickly turned to intense pleasure before additional light pressure on her anal passage had her gasping once more. Something else was being forced inside her. Staying completely still, she tried to evade the object by clenching herself as tightly as possible.

Mark thrust two fingers inside the trainee once more, found the elusive G-spot on the front wall of her vagina and started rubbing enthusiastically. In a few short seconds it achieved the desired effect. She couldn't keep her body tightly clenched when she was on the knife-edge of release. In a single thrust he part pushed, part forced the slippery object inside her. In this particular instance it was a kindness to be quick.

Not that she was going to thank him for it.

Jenny didn't scream. Although the sound bubbled up inside her she forced it back down again, unwilling to give them the satisfaction of hearing it. It hurt. It bloody hurt. Her sphincter was contracting madly around the device, whatever it was and it *hurt*. That didn't seem to matter though, because the sensation had nearly pushed her over the edge into what promised to be the mother of all orgasms. Her body hummed, throbbed, pulsed and shivered. Just the tiniest touch would send her tumbling. As soon as she thought her body had taken the path of no return, the stimulation stopped. All of it ceased at once. Not a hand, finger or tongue moved. If Jenny had thought denying these three strangers the pleasure of her release would hurt them, she'd had no idea how much it would actually hurt her. Her body trembled helplessly as the agony of sexual frustration overtook every pore. She was unable to hold back a sob of torment and a single tear slid down her cheek. As her chest heaved up and down with the effort needed to draw in breath, she felt her whole body ache with an indescribable pain.

In the background, Agnes sniffed. 'She's going to be a beauty.'

Hetty just shook her head, thinking of all the work that had to be done to get this trainee's tack ready in double time.

'Right, that's enough of Mr Nice Guy,' said Mark, giving the small butt plug inside Jenny's ass a little twist. He was rewarded with a grunt and a shudder. The plug had a little tube connected to it which could be used to pump it up in size, which he'd put to very good use later. For now, the slimmest size was more than adequate. 'You're mine for the next three hours and most of them will consist of the ingenious punishments I have been ordered to carry out. You've been a *very* naughty pony.' A wicked gleam lit up his expression.

Through her painful inhalations Jenny's eyes widened. She'd only been here an hour, two at the most. What could she have possibly managed to do wrong in that time?

'We need to come to an understanding on the matters of lateness, being rude, swearing, and there is also a stolen credit card that needs to be accounted for.' The riding crop on Master Mark's belt twitched with enthusiasm.

Oh Hell, thought Jenny in dismay; if that was Mr Nice Guy, she wasn't at all sure she wanted to meet Mr Nasty...

Enjoy more Pony Tales...

...in Book Two of Jenny's adventures, **Learning the Ropes**, also available as a paperback on **AMAZON**.

Finding a suitable four inch collar, he released the leather restraint around her neck. Gently bunching her long black hair into a ponytail, to ensure it didn't get trapped inside, he quickly fastened the two silver buckles at the rear that would hold it in place. Mark decided that was quite enough of the softly-softly approach. He tugged her hair sharply to get her attention and was rewarded with a grimace of pain. Her glorious blue eyes looked at him and widened like saucers as he spoke...

In Book Two of Pony Tales, Jenny finds herself in the capable hands of Mark, her guide and tormentor for the day. She becomes accomplished in the art of crawling, gets an eye-opening tour of the facility and suffers regularly with the pain of orgasm denial. Finding herself at the mercy of his fingertips, when he demonstrates the complexities of breath play, she panics that each gasp of air may be her last.

Displayed, touched, fondled and at the mercy of others, Jenny begins to discover what life as a pony girl might entail, especially when faced with the wicked tongues of several pony boys! Getting acquainted with the rather aptly named Red Room and finding herself subject to a thorough spanking is her first discovery into the delicious world of pain and pleasure that awaits her.

But there are far more devilish torments than spanking to be found at the Albrecht stables...